BONANZA

BONANZA

THE
BUBBLE GUM
KID

by

George S. Elrick

Authorized Edition

WHITMAN PUBLISHING COMPANY
Racine, Wisconsin

CONTENTS

"Apache Jack's Out to Kill You!"

Chapter 1

ENTER THE
BUBBLE GUM KID

"Apache Jack broke loose last week," announced the grizzled store manager, shifting a plug of chewing tobacco to the other side of his mouth. "He's out to kill all three of you Cartwrights!"

Little Joe patted the butt of his six-shooter. "That's why I'm wearing this peacemaker. I don't aim to be another notch on that cattle rustler's gun!"

Hoss Cartwright shouldered Little Joe to one side and looked squarely at the store manager. "We didn't come all the way into town to make conversation, Sam. We came to buy some feed for our stock."

The store manager tilted back his head and looked up at the huge figure towering over him. "How come *you* aren't packin' a gun, Hoss?"

"I figure I don't need one," replied Little Joe's big brother.

Hoss Isn't Afraid

"When it comes to trouble, I'd rather rely on my fists." He stared at his oversize hands. "They're just as effective at close range, anyway!" He threw back his head and laughed heartily.

"Not against Apache Jack," muttered the store manager. "He'll fill you full of holes before you get close enough to use your fists. I think Little Joe's got the right idea!"

"Be that as it may," said Little Joe, pulling the brim of his hat

"I'll Rely on My Fists!"

down over his forehead, "we need ten bags of feed. Why don't you have Injun Pete load 'em on our buckboard for us?"

"Okay," agreed Sam, working the tobacco back and forth in his mouth. He turned to an old Indian quietly puffing on a clay pipe in the corner. "Pete! Pile ten bags of feed on the Cartwright wagon. It's out in front by the hitching post."

The Indian grunted, smiled at the two Cartwright brothers with his coal-black eyes, and shuffled off

Injun Pete Puffs on His Pipe

to the storage room. "Me get-um for you," he said agreeably.

"We'd better get goin', Hoss," said Little Joe, turning on his heels and striding toward the door.

"I hope I see you boys again, but I kinda doubt it," called out the storekeeper, scratching the back of his head. "Not with Apache Jack slinking around in the tall timber, hankerin' to take a potshot at you."

"Hey, you're right!" exclaimed Hoss, wiping his brawny hands on his leather vest. "One of us had

"We'd Better Go, Hoss."

better gallop down the trail and warn Pa before he finishes biddin' for that lumber contract in the next town. He'll be a sittin' duck ridin' back by himself through the woods!"

Little Joe turned his head to say something, unaware of a short, skinny figure in a bright red shirt suddenly blocking the doorway. His shoulder smashed into the stranger's small chest, knocking him backward against the rickety porch railing in front of the store. The railing

Accidental Collision

fell apart with a crackling sound, and the red-shirted youth fell over backward and sprawled awkwardly in the dusty street.

"Take it easy, Joseph!" warned Hoss. "You tryin' to get into a fight, just 'cause you're wearin' a gun?"

"I didn't see him!" protested Little Joe. "I guess I'd better apologize."

"Forget the apologies! Just reach for the sky!" snarled the stranger, shaking the dust out of his shaggy blond hair as he staggered to his

Snarling Stranger

feet and fumbled for his Colt .45.

"Reach, my eye!" answered Little Joe in an angry voice. "Who do you think you are, junior? Last of the big-time outlaws?"

"Nobody pushes the Bubble Gum Kid around!" panted the stranger, shoving the muzzle of his gun into Little Joe's stomach. He immediately squeezed the trigger.

Instead of sinking to his knees with a bullet lodged in his vitals, Little Joe merely licked his lips. The gun had failed to fire.

"Nobody Pushes Me Around!"

"Let the little varmint have it!" snorted Hoss from the store steps.

Hoss was wasting his breath, however, for Little Joe needed no advice. He knocked the gun from the stranger's trembling fingers with a lightning movement of his left hand, then kicked it thirty feet down the street. A split second later, the knotted fist of his right hand sledgehammered into the stranger's jaw.

The Bubble Gum Kid swayed back and forth on his feet, rolled

A Right to the Jaw

his baby-blue eyes, and collapsed like a deflated balloon.

"I have half a mind to lay that whippersnapper across my knee and thrash him!" muttered Hoss, picking up the unconscious youth's revolver, snapping open the cylinder, and emptying the cartridges into his hand. He stared at the weapon through narrowed eyes. "No wonder it didn't fire!" he exclaimed. "It looks like it was made from leftover tin cans!"

Little Joe rubbed the back of his

Down and Out

right hand. "I didn't mean to clout him that hard," he said. "It took the skin off my knuckles!"

"Your wagon's ready," interjected Injun Pete, still calmly puffing on his clay pipe. He glanced down at the figure spread-eagled in the center of the street. "You hit-um plenty hard," he murmured. Then, without a backward glance, he shuffled back into the general store.

"What'll we do with this idiot?" asked Little Joe, nudging the red-

Skinned Knuckles

shirted stranger with the toe of his boot. "Shouldn't we drag him over into the shade?"

"Aw-w-w-w, he'll be all right," replied Hoss, climbing up into the driver's seat of the buckboard.

"What if he tries to shoot some-one else?" Little Joe asked as he climbed up beside his brother.

Hoss chuckled and took the reins in his hands. "He's as harmless as a newborn infant with that two-bit pistol of his. The only danger is it might explode in his hand!"

"He'll Be All Right!"

Rattling Across the Prairie

Chapter 2

SHADOW IN THE NIGHT

Scattering wild-eyed jackrabbits and kicking up clouds of yellow dust into the evening breeze, the Cartwright buckboard rattled across the bumpy prairie toward the pine-covered foothills leading up to their combination logging camp and ranch, which was known to every white man, Indian, and half-breed as "The Ponderosa."

Little Joe drummed his fingers against his leather holster. "Suppose Apache Jack's waitin' for us up at the cabin? I can see him now, swilling down a cup of Hop Sing's scalding black coffee. . . ."

". . . which would burn the lining out of his dirty throat!" finished Hoss.

"And he's probably facing the front door with a cocked Winchester on his lap!" continued Little Joe.

"Suppose Apache Jack's Waiting for Us?"

"It's not *us* I'm worried about—it's Pa!" mused Hoss. "After all, it was Pa who ran Apache Jack out of town after bustin' his ugly nose!"

"And smashing his two pistols against a rock!" remembered Little Joe.

"I'll never forget it," Hoss continued. What a fist fight! He told Apache Jack to make tracks before sundown, or the town's citizens would string him up at a necktie party!"

Hoss and Little Joe Reminisce

The buckboard lurched into a wagon rut and creaked upward through the first stand of timber.

"Ya know," said Hoss thoughtfully, a note of admiration in his voice, "I'd rather face a wounded mountain lion than Pa when he's caught someone rustlin' his best beef!"

"Hey! What's that paper tacked on the tree over there?" asked Little Joe suddenly clapping his hand on his brother's enormous wrist. Hoss pulled back on the reins and the

"What's That Over There?"

horses stopped in their tracks.

Joseph Cartwright leaped down from the buckboard seat and examined the tattered sign.

"What does it say?" asked Hoss, impatient to get back to the cabin.

"It says, 'Wanted — Dead or Alive'!" read Little Joe out loud.

"*Who*, wanted dead or alive, and for *what?*" demanded Hoss.

"Just name it, Hoss, and you'll find it listed here," answered Little Joe. "It says, 'Look out for the Bubble Gum Kid. Run out of Dodge

An Ominous Poster

City for cattle rustling, bank robbery, stagecoach holdups, and several killings!"

"Lemme see that face!" said Hoss, climbing down from his seat. He stared at the poster. "Say, isn't this the punk you just knocked cold in front of the general store?"

"Well, I'll be danged!" said Little Joe.

"Maybe the skinny little hombre isn't as harmless as we think he is!" mused Hoss.

"Are you kidding?" exclaimed

"Well, I'll Be Danged!"

Little Joe. "I tapped him on the jaw just once and he went down like a buffalo with an arrow in its spine. He's a fake, I tell ya! He couldn't thrash his way out of a wet paper bag!"

"Maybe that's why he pulls that useless pistol on everybody," mused Hoss, climbing back into the rickety seat on top of the buckboard. "Probably makes the spindly-legged stripling feel like a man!"

Little Joe climbed back on the seat as Hoss again flipped the reins

Hoss Flips the Reins

up and down. The tired horses trotted forward, eager to get back to the corral.

"He'd better watch his step," said Joe. "There are some pretty tough characters in this neck of the woods who aren't wanted by the law. I know cowpunchers and lumberjacks who wouldn't hesitate to take him apart."

Hoss chuckled, in spite of his deep concern for his father, who, he knew, even now might be cantering into an ambush or lying dead

The Horses Trot Forward

in the bushes, a bullet in his back. "I'd like to see that skinny little runt shoot it out with a gunslick like Apache Jack!"

Little Joe grinned, his teeth glinting white in the dusk. "He'd look like a chicken-wire fence before he could yank that toy gun out of his belt! Apache Jack doesn't even bother to squeeze the trigger. He simply fans the hammer with the back of his other hand!" The grin suddenly faded from his face. "What are we jokin' about? Pa's

"Apache Jack <u>Fans</u> the Hammer!"

in real danger unless I gallop down the trail and warn him that Apache Jack's waitin' for him."

"Pep it up, you lazy critters!" snapped Hoss, slapping the reins up and down. The horses strained forward. Hoss turned to his kid brother. "*I'll* ride down the trail and warn Pa. You keep guard over Hop Sing and the cabin."

The buckboard slammed around the last turn in the trail and rolled through the open front gate of the Ponderosa. A kerosene lamp burned

Back at the Ponderosa

quietly in the window. Smoke curled upward from the massive stone chimney. Hop Sing, the Cartwright's Oriental cook, appeared in the doorway, a cast-iron frying pan in his hand. "You velly late!" he exclaimed, his eight-inch pigtail bobbing up and down.

Little Joe jumped to the ground and started to unhitch the horses. Hoss lumbered into the barn to saddle up the black mare. "Anything happen while we were gone?" asked the youngest Cartwright.

Hop Sing Appears

"Velly quiet!" replied the cook. "Where is Mister Hoss going? It velly dark!"

"He's gonna ride to the next town to warn Pa!" replied Little Joe, patting the two weary horses on the rump as they shuffled forward to the watering trough. "Apache Jack broke out of jail and is gunnin' for all of us!"

Hop Sing dropped his frying pan on his foot and began to leap around as though he'd broken a toe or two. "Apache Jack? He a bad man?"

Hop Sing Hops

"The bottom of the barrel!" replied Little Joe as Hoss burst out of the barn and galloped off into the night. "Better get out of that doorway, Hop Sing! He'd pick *you* off just for the fun of it!"

Hop Sing pulled back into the shadows, his face strained with fear.

"Douse that light!" said Little Joe as he entered the cabin. "And put out the fire! Apache Jack can't hit what he can't see."

The faithful houseboy pursed his

"Douse That Light!"

lips, blew out the light, and splashed a bucket of soapy water on the fireplace logs. Little Joe turned to him. "Can you handle a gun?" he demanded.

"Me not handle gun!" whimpered Hop Sing. "Me only handle flying pan!"

"Well, get some sleep," advised Joe, rotating the cylinder of his revolver to make certain all six chambers contained shells.

Silence settled down on the cabin. The only audible sound was Hop

Little Joe Checks His Gun

Sing's labored breathing and the soft crunching of Little Joe's teeth as he nibbled on a piece of hardtack. As the hours dragged by, Joe's head nodded and his chin rested on his chest.

Only the horses in the stable were aware of a shadowy figure which appeared by the gate, pistol in hand. An owl in a nearby tree blinked solemnly as the sinister shape crept toward the cabin door.

A Sinister Shape

Little Joe Awakes With a Start

Chapter 3

RETURN OF THE KID

Little Joe awoke with a nervous start. A shaft of sunlight had forced its way through the dusty windowpane and was tickling his eyelids. He shook his head, brushed the hardtack crumbs from his lap, and glanced around the room. Hop Sing was still snoring in the corner, the frying pan tightly clutched in one hand. Joe automatically reached for the revolver he had placed on the table the night before.

"Hey! *Someone stole my gun!*" he exclaimed, leaping to his feet and knocking over his chair.

Hop Sing opened his eyes and blinked. "Time for bleakfast!" he said, a wide grin creasing his leathery face.

The remark fell on deaf ears. Little Joe had exploded through the cabin door and was half-crouching in the center of the porch, his head

"Someone Stole My Gun!"

swiveling back and forth. "Dad blast it! Nobody can steal my gun and get away with it!"

Hop Sing appeared in the doorway. "Nobody swipe your gun, Mister Joseph! Your pistol here on the floor!" He stooped down and picked up a metallic object, holding it gingerly between his thumb and forefinger as though it were a poisonous snake.

"Lemme see that gun!" Little Joe sprang forward and jerked the revolver out of Hop Sing's hands.

"Here Your Pistol!"

"This isn't my gun! This is the kind of toy gun you give little boys for Christmas!"

"What this on door?" asked the cook, nervously pointing to a sheet of paper that fluttered in the breeze.

"Well, I'll be fried in chicken fat!" Little Joe ripped the sheet of paper from the wood planks and stared at it. It was a duplicate of the WANTED—DEAD OR ALIVE sign he had discovered tacked to the tree when riding the buckboard back from town with Hoss.

A Duplicate Poster

"You got gooey pink stuff on fingers!" pointed out Hop Sing.

Joe studied his hands, a look of disgust twisting his features. Two wads of well-chewed gum were holding his fingers together like glue. "So that's what he used to fasten the paper to the door! The Bubble Gum Kid must be a *nut!*"

"Nobody calls the Bubble Gum Kid a nut!"

Little Joe spun around and found himself staring down the barrel of his own gun. The red-shirted

"Nobody Calls Me a Nut!"

youngster he had knocked down in town stared back at him with pale blue eyes. Wisps of hay dangling from his hair indicated he had spent the night in the barn. Methodically working a stick of gum back and forth between his lips and his tongue, the Bubble Gum Kid blew an enormous bubble, popped it, and pulled the trigger. A flash of flame and smoke shattered the air. The bullet zinged past Little Joe's ear and splintered the door.

"You're not going to shoot me

A Near Miss

down in cold blood, are you?" asked Little Joe, biting his lower lip.

"Draw!" barked his foe. "You've got a gun in your hand!"

"This isn't a gun!" replied young Cartwright, examining the flimsy pistol the Kid had secretly swapped with him. "This is nothing but pieces of metal held together with baling wire!"

"Tough luck!" replied the Kid, squeezing the trigger again. Another flash of flame tore through the air. The acrid smell of burnt

"This Isn't a Gun!"

powder wafted to Little Joe's nostrils. The bullet had missed him by a country mile.

"You'd better give me that, junior, before you hurt yourself!" commented Little Joe.

The Bubble Gum Kid stepped back and carefully popped another pink bubble. "I told you to draw! This is the wild and woolly West, where scores are settled with cold steel and hot lead!"

"You've been reading too many dime novels, sonny!" said Little

"Draw!"

Joe, reluctantly raising the dilapidated gun. He squeezed the trigger and the revolver fell apart in his hand.

"Let's get this over with!" gasped the Kid, looking faintly sheepish. He fired three more shots at Little Joe in rapid succession. One bullet whined past Joe's left ear and flipped a shingle from the roof. Another plunked into a fence post, showering slivers in all directions. The third plowed into the ground at Little Joe's feet.

The Revolver Blew Apart

"I must be losing my touch," muttered the Bubble Gum Kid, beads of perspiration breaking out on his forehead, a half-formed bubble hanging from his lips.

"You've got one shot left!" said Little Joe in a flat voice. "If you miss with that one, I'm gonna finish the job I started in town when I knocked you off the porch!"

The Kid raised the stolen Colt .45 with a trembling hand, stepped forward, and shoved the muzzle point-blank into Little Joe's broad chest.

The Kid Grows Nervous

His hand shook so violently that the barrel wobbled back and forth, ripping off one of Joe's buttons. For a long moment, neither breathed.

"I can't do it!" blurted out the Kid at last. "I'm just a big fake!"

Little Joe lifted him from the ground with an uppercut that snapped his teeth together. The Bubble Gum Kid flopped backward and lay still in the dust.

"He lousy shot!" observed Hop Sing, peering around the corner.

"Crazy nut!" said Little Joe,

The Kid Hits the Dust

rubbing the back of his knuckles.
He reached down, scooped up his
revolver, and snapped open the cylinder. The one remaining bullet
dropped out and rolled over in the
grass. "If Apache Jack had seen
this showdown he would have split
his britches laughing!"

"What's goin' on, Joseph?"

Little Joe wheeled around. Pa
Cartwright and Hoss were side by
side in the entranceway to the corral, Hoss on his black mare, Pa on
the scrubby roan he favored.

"What's Goin' On?"

The youngest Cartwright shrugged his shoulders helplessly. "Looks like we've picked up a maverick to end all mavericks, Pa."

Hoss dismounted and strolled over to the fallen figure. "Why, it's that goofy Bubble Gum Kid again!"

"We'd better tie his wrists to his ankles," ventured Little Joe, blowing on the back of his knuckles. "Otherwise he's liable to hurt himself. Then I'm gonna drag this little squirt to town and collect the reward money!"

Little Joe Explains

Ben Examines The Kid

Chapter 4

THE KID IS FOUND OUT

"What's that hanging out of the corner of his mouth?" asked Ben Cartwright, examining the bruised jaw of the unconscious Bubble Gum Kid.

"Aw . . . it's just a special kind of gum," replied Little Joe, making a wry face. "This nitwit chews it all the time. He even blew bubbles

with it when he was takin' potshots
at me with my own gun!" Rolling
the Kid over on his stomach, Joe
lashed his hands together with a
rawhide thong.

"What are ya plannin' to do with
the reward money, Joe?" asked
Hoss, tilting his floppy hat back on
his sunburned forehead.

The Bubble Gum Kid groaned
groggily, then mumbled softly,
"There ain't no reward money."

"What do you mean, no reward
money!" demanded Little Joe, as he

The Kid Is Tied Up

tightened the thong and flipped the lightweight captive over on his back. "It *says* so on the 'Wanted—Dead or Alive' sign you plastered on our front door!"

The Kid shook his head in a dazed manner, then averted his gaze so he wouldn't have to look Little Joe in the eye. "That sign is as phony as a six-dollar bill. I had it printed up myself, with my own money."

"Well, I'll be a two-headed mustang!" exclaimed Hoss, whistling

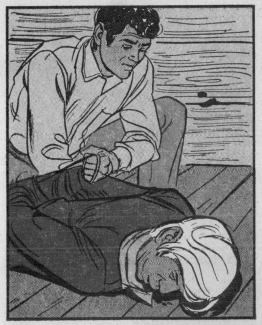

Little Joe Tightened the Thong

through his teeth. "You *are* a strange one! Where are ya from, son?"

"Chicago," answered the Kid. "I'm a city boy who always hankered to come West. Trouble is, I can't even sit on a horse. I fell off twelve times ridin' up here."

"If you rode a horse up here, where is it?" muttered Little Joe.

The Kid struggled to sit up. "Over there, behind your barn."

"I'm gonna take a look at it," said Hoss, clomping off.

"I'm Gonna Look at That Horse!"

Ben stared at the gun that had fallen apart in Little Joe's hands and now lay scattered in the grass. A frown wrinkled his forehead. "Where'd you get *that* peashooter?" he asked curiously.

"From a trader I met in town. I think his name was Honest Dollar Harry. He also sold me my cayuse."

Ben chuckled in spite of himself. "Honest Dollar Harry would double-cross his own grandmother if he could get away with it," he told the boy.

Ben Stares at the Scattered Gun Parts

"You mean I've been fleeced?"

"By an expert! Harry's crooked as a deer's antlers. He'd skin a mosquito for its fat. For your information, son, he's been tarred and feathered and run out of practically every town west of the Mississippi!"

The Kid narrowed his eyes. "I reckon I'd better shoot it out with the varmint!"

"Not the way *you* shoot!" commented Little Joe, a faint smile turning up the corners of his

"You Mean I've Been Fleeced?"

mouth. "We'll take care of Honest Dollar Harry for you. Eh, Pa?"

"Right, Joseph."

"This is no horse!" shouted Hoss from behind the barn. "It looks more like a broken-down moose cow!"

"Examine its teeth to see how old it is," suggested Pa.

There was a moment of silence. Then came the verdict, "It hasn't *got* any teeth!"

Something crackled in the bushes. Ben Cartwright spun around,

"This Is No Horse!"

yanking his Colt from its holster.

As a chipmunk poked its head through the leaves and then vanished, the Bubble Gum Kid finally whispered, "You sure can slap your hardware. I couldn't even *see* your hand!" He paused. "You men expectin' trouble?"

"Rattlesnake trouble," commented Hoss, rejoining them. "Ever hear of a low-down critter named Apache Jack?"

"I was aimin' to kill him!" replied the Kid.

Ben Draws His Colt

The Cartwrights stared open-mouthed at their captive. "*You* were gonna plug Apache Jack?" Hoss finally asked in astonishment.

"Yer darn tootin'!" replied the Kid, staggering to his feet, his wrists still tied behind his back.

"Untie him!" commanded Ben.

"You make about as much sense as a crippled prairie dog attackin' a grizzly bear!" exclaimed Hoss, slapping his hands on his knees. "Why were *you* aimin' to knock him off?"

"<u>You</u> Plug Apache Jack?"

"I came West to make a name for myself," said the Kid, working his wad of gum between his teeth and his tongue. "I'm an orphan. Never had a father to look after me. Seems like I've been pushed around all my life."

"So?" questioned Ben.

"So I decided to come West to shoot things up. I figured it was time to show everybody how tough I really am!"

Hop Sing stepped out of the cabin doorway clanging an iron soup

The Kid Tells His Story

spoon against a battered kettle. "Time for bleakfast! Flapjacks on table!"

Ben Cartwright placed his hand on the Bubble Gum Kid's shoulder, wincing as the Kid popped a bubble. "How about some grub, Kid? When's the last time you had chow under your belt?"

"To tell ya the honest truth, I haven't eaten anything except a handful of acorns for two days . . . *Pa.*" He and Ben exchanged a long, meaningful glance.

"How About Some Grub, Kid?"

As the four men trailed single file into the cabin, Little Joe took a last backward glance over his shoulder. "I wonder when Apache Jack's gonna start blasting away at us?" he murmured.

"Not for a couple of days, Joseph," replied Ben.

The Cartwrights and their guest sat down at the crude table, grabbed their knives and forks, and hacked away at the pancakes piled high on each plate.

"How come?" asked Hoss.

A Hungry Guest

"Since there's more than one Cartwright to bump off, he's probably gatherin' a gang of fellow cutthroats to help him. Remember what I've always told you, Hoss—all hard-boiled eggs are yellow inside!"

"That's a good one, Pa!" said the Bubble Gum Kid, stuffing his mouth with an enormous forkful. He waved his table knife at Little Joe. "I hope you ain't sore at me, Little Joe, because I tried to fill you full of holes!"

"I Hope You Ain't Sore!"

"No, I'm not sore at you," replied the youngest Cartwright in a flat, unfriendly voice, remembering how he'd been cheated out of any reward money. "Just keep away from me . . . that's all! I'm gettin' sick and tired of punching you in the jaw!"

"Just Keep Away From Me!"

Apache Jack

Chapter 5

MORE TROUBLE BREWING

Apache Jack spat a stream of tobacco into the small, Indian-style fire that sputtered before him. The fire's embers cast an eerie glow on the damp walls of the cave. "Shut up, Yellow Wolf!" he snarled. "I don't need your advice."

The Red Man's hand streaked for the bowie knife that glistened on a tattered blanket roll. "You tell me shut up too much!"

With a coarse laugh Apache Jack smashed the toe of his scuffed boot into the downward-flashing wrist. Grunting in pain, the Indian jerked his fingers open. The knife clattered against a rocky ledge and fell to the ground.

"I'll slaughter them Cartwrights when I'm good 'n' ready . . . and I'm not ready yet!" he snarled.

Yellow Wolf exhaled his breath slowly, then settled back on his

Jack Kicks the Knife Away

striped blanket as though nothing had happened. He prodded the fire with his heel. "Why we wait so long? Why you have Buffalo Face spy on 'em all the time?"

"I want the Cartwrights to think I've left the area," replied the coarse-faced rustler in a low voice. "I want 'em to be completely off guard, 'cause I have special plans for killing 'em!"

Yellow Wolf glanced around the cramped cave. "We got three Winchesters 'n' plenty bullets. You

"Why We Wait So Long?"

wear two six-guns on belt. Why we not just walk up and blow 'em full of holes? You still the fastest draw in the West!"

Apache Jack removed one of his pistols and spun the cylinder. "This gun's okay for killin' a horse with a broken leg . . . but it's too good for the Cartwrights!"

The Indian leaned forward, his beady eyes glistening. "Me remember how you scalped two men alive! You gonna scalp Ben Cartwright?"

"Maybe!"

"I Have Other Plans!"

The renegade savage grinned in anticipation.

"But, first, I'm gonna surprise the Cartwrights—as soon as that skinny kid who's stayin' with 'em leaves—'n' tie 'em up on the backs of their horses."

"Ha! Then we shoot 'em?"

"No, I want to drag this thing out as long as I can. I haven't had any fun since I broke out of jail."

"What we do next?"

"Remember how old Ben Cartwright threatened to have me

"I'm Gonna Surprise the Cartwrights!"

strung up on a rope 'cause I was rustlin' his cattle?"

"Me remember! He smash your guns against rock!"

"Well, I'm gonna slowly string up all three Cartwrights . . . then use 'em for target practice while they're kickin' in midair. And I'm also gonna burn their cabin 'n' corral to the ground! How does *that* getcha?"

Yellow Wolf's frame shook with laughter. "Me like!"

Apache Jack slid the Colt he was

Yellow Wolf Shakes With Laughter

fingering back into its holster. "But we have to wait till that kid with the red shirt leaves, 'cause there are four of 'em now, 'n' only three of us. Ol' Apache Jack doesn't like bein' outnumbered!"

The muffled padding of a horse's hooves caught their attention. Yellow Wolf slapped his hand on the nearest Winchester, and Apache Jack drew both six-shooters, ready to fire with deadly accuracy. Both faced the threadbare blanket that served as a makeshift curtain at

Ready For the Intruder

the narrow entrance to the cave. In a moment the blanket parted and a beefy Indian appeared, breathing heavily. It was Buffalo Face.

"I keep tellin' ya to let us know who you are before pushin' through that blanket!" warned Apache Jack. "Otherwise you're liable to end up with a bullet in that blubbery stomach of yours!"

Buffalo Face stared without expression at the two men, then flopped down on the floor of the cave. "Me tired!"

Buffalo Face Appears

"What were they doin' today?" asked Apache Jack.

"Let me catch breath," said Buffalo Face.

"Come on! We've been cooped up in this cold cave all day! What were they doin'?" snarled Apache Jack.

"Well," replied the tribal outcast, who, in the firelight, resembled a weary hippopotamus, "all skinny kid does is fire gun . . . again and again!"

"What do ya mean, fire a gun? Ya told me he didn't even know how

A Report on the Ponderosa

to *hold* a gun the right way!"

"He learn fast!"

"Who's teachin' him?"

"Little Joe."

Apache Jack exchanged glances with Yellow Wolf. "You're lyin'! You told me two days ago that Little Joe wouldn't even talk to that scrawny runt!"

"Now he talk to him all the time. They become plenty good friends!"

An ember shifted in the dying fire, throwing up a shower of sparks.

"You're Lyin'!"

"Listen!" said Buffalo Face, cupping a pudgy hand to one ear. "He still firing gun . . . even in dark!"

Apache Jack and Yellow Wolf cocked their heads to one side. "I don't hear nuthin'!" Apache Jack muttered.

"Go to mouth of cave 'n' listen!"

The long-haired rustler stood up, brushed his greasy denims, and walked to the cave entrance, stooping over so as not to bang his head against rock outcroppings. He pushed the tattered blanket to one

Apache Jack Steps Out

side and stepped out into the moonlight.

In the distance a faint *pop* shivered through the cold night air. Nearby ledges bounced the soft echo back and forth. Five more *pops* followed in rapid succession.

Apache Jack frowned. "That kid had better make tracks fast! He's gettin too handy with shootin' irons."

He Hears Gunshots

Ben Grits His Teeth

Chapter 6

SHOOTING LESSONS

A volley of shots rattled the early morning air.

Ben Cartwright, sipping from a mug of scalding hot coffee, gritted his teeth.

Hop Sing, who had been stoking a fire in the potbellied stove, paused long enough to cram a cotton ball into each ear.

"Dad blast it!" shouted Ben, slamming down the mug on the rough-hewn table. "Sometimes I wish Little Joe hadn't given the Kid his old pistol!"

"Take it easy, Pa," said Hoss, grinning in spite of himself. "It's better than listenin' to him pop that crazy gum!"

"Maybe," said Ben, hastily dabbing at the coffee he had spilled. "But it sounds like the Battle of Gettysburg out there—all day and all night!"

"Dad Blast It!"

"Mister Joseph not eat bleakfast again!" said Hop Sing. "He too busy showing Bubble Gum Kid how to shoot!"

Ben made a wry face and nodded his head. "The Kid blasts away at pine cones, tin cans, old horseshoes . . . *anything!* Amazingly enough, he's gettin' so he hits what he's shootin' at!"

"Why don't we put the Kid to work?" suggested Hoss.

"Doin' what?" asked Ben, wincing again as another volley of shots

"It's Little Joe and The Kid!"

shook dead leaves from the trees.

"Choppin' wood," replied Hoss.

"Do you think any underfed orphan kid raised on city streets is strong enough to swing an ax?"

"*Strong* enough!" snorted Hoss. "Do you know that punk's eaten thirty-five flapjacks every day for the past two weeks? I'll bet a pair of Mexican spurs he's gained twelve pounds!"

Ben picked up a heavy, double-edged ax as they stepped out of the cabin. "We'll soon see if he can

"We'll Let The Kid Chop Some Wood!"

twirl this as easily as he twirls that six-shooter!"

"They're behind the barn," said Hoss. "They're givin' our milk cow a nervous breakdown with all that gunfire!" He chuckled softly. "Why don't we kinda creep up on 'em 'n' see what fancy tricks Little Joe is teachin'?"

While Buffalo Face shifted his bulky body into a more restful position, squinting his eyes and watching every movement from the protection of a nearby ledge, Ben and

A Spy on a Nearby Ledge

Hoss silently shuffled forward through the pine needles. Quietly flattening themselves against peeling paint on the far side of the barn, they strained their ears to hear what Little Joe and the Bubble Gum Kid were saying.

"Now, watch how I twist my wrist," instructed Little Joe. "This is known as the 'road agent's spin,' and it's a great way to rip a hole through your own stomach if you're not careful!"

"So, what's it used for?" asked

The Road Agent's Spin

the Kid, casually popping his gum.

"If some hombre gets the drop on you and asks you to fork over your gun—with the butt toward him and the barrel facing your own middle. . . ."

"I follow you," said the Kid.

"You *start* to hand your gun to him, the way he asked."

"Yeah, I see!"

"Then you suddenly spin it around on your index finger, which you've been careful to keep in the trigger guard."

The Kid Learns Fast

The Kid started to blow a bubble.

"And, before the other guy knows what's happened, your gun barrel's pressed against his ribs, and you've got the drop on *him*."

"Lemme try it!" said the gum-chewing youth, taking the glistening weapon from Little Joe and artfully spinning it several times. "Nuthin' to it!"

"You keep on shootin'," replied the youngest Cartwright, hitching his thumbs into his belt. "I'm gonna pack some grub into my middle.

"Lemme Try It!"

Ever since I started teachin' you how to be a freewheeling gunslick I haven't eaten enough food to put in a brook trout's ear!"

The Bubble Gum Kid hefted the gun in his hand. He hesitated for a moment, then blurted out, "How's Pa doin' this morning?"

"Just fine, I reckon," answered Joe, walking toward the corner of the barn. "You sure do think a lot of him, don't you?"

"Sure do," replied the Kid, softly popping his gum. "Never had a

"Just Keep Practicing!"

pa of my own, ya know."

"I know." said Little Joe, shrugging his shoulders. "Sometimes you look at him as if you were a longhorn starved for salt!"

The Bubble Gum Kid stopped chewing the pink wad in his mouth for a moment, turned, and started firing at pine cones dangling from a nearby tree. One by one, they disintegrated into brown powder.

"Say, Kid!" exclaimed Hoss, striding around the corner of the barn.

Pine Cones for Targets

The Kid slipped his smoking pistol into its holster. "Yeah, Hoss?"

"We've been thinkin'. . . ." Suddenly at a loss for words, Hoss turned to his father.

Ben arched his shaggy eyebrows, then held out the ax to the Kid. "Ever use one of these?" he asked.

The Kid pulled back as if he'd been handed a smoking bomb that might explode in his face. "You mean you want me to *work?*"

"That's right," answered Ben. "No, thanks," said the Kid in a

"You Want Me to <u>Work</u>?"

strange voice. He backed up, slowly, his jaw muscles twitching. He looked Ben in the eye uneasily. "I'm a *gunman* . . . not a *woodchopper!*" Spinning on his heels, he stalked toward his toothless horse. Ben Cartwright's face sagged with disappointment.

High up on the ledge, Buffalo Face grunted to himself. "Me tellum Apache Jack the Bubble Gum Kid leave! Now we kill all three Cartwrights!" His fat bronze face twisted into an evil grin.

"Me Tell-um Apache Jack!"

The Kid Saddles Up

Chapter 7

TROUBLE AHEAD

"Where ya aimin' to go?" Little Joe asked the Bubble Gum Kid in a strained voice as Ben dropped the ax on the ground, turned, and walked back toward the cabin. The Kid threw a saddle on the back of his swaybacked horse. The animal's legs immediately buckled under the leathery weight.

"Mexico!" replied the Kid, adjusting one of the stirrups. "I think I'll head for the border 'n' shoot it up down there!"

"That's a long way from here!" said Hoss, glaring at the Kid through narrowed eyes, his beefy hands on his hips. "When do ya think you'll get there?"

"In a couple of weeks," replied the Kid, working his gum back and forth. "I'll bet a Confederate dollar nobody's gonna ask me to chop logs down *there!*"

"I'll Head for Mexico!"

"You birdbrain—you won't even be out of the local *woods* in two weeks!" snorted Little Joe.

"Maybe," retorted the Kid, swinging up into his saddle and almost sliding off on the other side. "But don't fret about me. Nobody ever has. I'm the kinda hombre that can stomp his own snakes!"

"Even a gunfighter can't stomp rattlers on an empty stomach!" called out Ben in a flat voice as he emerged from the darkness of the cabin door with a tattered blanket

Unsteady Rider

roll in his arms. "I've asked Hop
Sing to put enough dried beef in
this roll to last you for three days.
That should be enough to get you
out of this mountain country down
to the flat lands. Then you can
sponge off Indian settlements as
you head south."

Hoss shrugged his shoulders. "I
don't know why you bother with
this ungrateful punk, Pa. When I
think of all the flapjacks he's stuffed
into his stomach, it makes me see
red!" He spat in the dust.

Food for the Trip

The Kid reached down, accepted the blanket roll, and folded it across his saddle. "Thanks, Pa," he murmured. He turned his face so as not to look Ben in the eye.

"Get goin'!" said Hoss. "And give that old six-shooter back to us before ya leave this corral!"

"Take it easy, Hoss," interjected Ben Cartwright. "That's no way to act! After all, the Kid's been our guest!"

The Kid removed the Colt .45 from his holster and handed it to

"You'll Need That Gun!"

Little Joe. "Here," he said quietly.

"Keep it!" muttered the youngest Cartwright. "You'll need it if you bump into Apache Jack up in the high timber."

"Fat chance!" remarked the Bubble Gum Kid under his breath. "Apache Jack's left these parts for good. Otherwise, he'd have shown up by *this* time!" Expertly slipping the revolver back into its holster, he spun his decrepit mount around and trotted awkwardly toward the corral gate.

The Kid Departs

The three Cartwrights watched in silence as the red-shirted figure swayed back and forth in his saddle. The Kid turned for a moment, waved his hand, then grabbed the pommel to regain his balance. Throwing up clouds of pine needles with its ancient hooves, the toothless cow pony clomped down the narrow trail that twisted through the scrub timber and vanished from sight.

"I still say that's a moose cow!" Hoss remarked.

Watching in Silence

"Anyway, he stays in the saddle better than he used to," said Little Joe.

While the Bubble Gum Kid trotted aimlessly toward the distant Mexican border, Buffalo Face silently led his black and white stallion away from its camouflaged hiding place near the Ponderosa. In a few moments he heaved his huge bulk on the horse's back and galloped toward Apache Jack's cave.

Apache Jack was waiting for the Indian at the cave entrance, his

Buffalo Face Steals Away

greasy black hair hanging straight down on each side of his swarthy face. "Has that gun-crazy squirt left?" he asked, twisting back his lips to reveal several broken teeth.

Buffalo Face slid from the horse's back and stood in front of his ringleader. "He leave just now . . . and he no come back. They have big argument! *Now* we string-um up and scalp-um, Apache Jack?"

The rustler ran the tip of his tongue along his chapped lower lip. "Now we'll do all sorts of things to

A Report on The Kid

'em . . . including *scalping!*" His eyes gleamed in anticipation. "Come on. Let's get our ropes and guns!"

Yellow Wolf, snoring heavily by the smoking fire in the center of the cave, woke with a yelp as Apache Jack gave him a savage kick in the ribs. "On your feet, you flea-bitten renegade. We're gonna have us some real fun!"

"I take ropes and my Winchester!" panted Buffalo Face, grasping the items indicated and turning

Awakened by a Savage Kick

toward the mouth of the cave once more.

"Wait a minute, Buffalo Face. That's *my* Winchester!" grunted Apache Jack, digging his cracked fingernails into Buffalo Face's shoulder. "Use yer *own* gun!"

"Me carve-um into little pieces!" whispered Yellow Wolf hoarsely, sliding a curved skinning knife into its sheath. "Here your knife!" he said to the outlaw, handing Apache Jack his wicked-looking bowie blade.

"Here Your Knife!"

"Shake a leg!" Apache Jack commanded, tossing a coiled rope over one shoulder. "I wanna see 'em kicking at the ends of these special neckties before the sun goes down tonight!"

Yellow Wolf unhitched his strawberry roan, slapped a dirty blanket on its back, and slipped a twisted hackamore around its mouth. "How we attack? I forget what you tell me."

"I ought to pump ya full of lead!" sneered Apache Jack, adjusting his

Preparing to Ride

saddle. "Can't ya ever remember anything?"

"He have no brains," commented Buffalo Face. "That's why he kicked out of tribe!"

"Me remember!" mumbled Yellow Wolf, wrestling with his confused thoughts. "We sneak up from three different sides."

"*When* they're out in the open and away from their guns!" the outlaw snarled. "And, when we get into position, don't do nuthin' till I fire my gun in the air!"

"He Have No Brains!"

The two savages nodded and lined up their ponies behind Apache Jack's. "Me like blood!" blurted out Yellow Wolf.

"You'll see plenty of it before this day's over!" muttered the greasy-haired rustler. He gestured with his hand, and they rode off in a silent single file, Winchesters cocked and trigger fingers itching.

Riding Off in Single File

"Things Are Gonna Be Quiet!"

Chapter 8

GUNFIGHT AT THE PONDEROSA

"Things are gonna be pretty quiet around here with that nitwit gone!" commented Little Joe.

"You're right as rain," said Hoss. "The crazy little maverick was always shootin' bullets or poppin' his gum. Durned if I know which was worse!"

"Well, boys, let's quit clackin'

our jaws together," exclaimed Ben, spitting into his hands and rubbing them together. "There's a heap of work to be done between now 'n' next Friday, when our new lumberjack crew shows up."

"Wait a minute, Pa," said Hoss, holding out a huge hand, his eyes darting back and forth warily. "Hear anythin' strange?"

"Cut the comedy, Hoss. I'm tired of pullin' my gun on chipmunks!" replied Ben, turning on his heels and striding toward the cabin.

Hoss Hears Something

The explosive crack of a Winchester tore through the silence.

"Since when have I been a crummy chipmunk?" Apache Jack's grimy face leered at them over the octagonal blue barrel of his rifle.

Little Joe lunged like a wildcat for his gun belt, which was dangling uselessly from a fence post. Apache Jack jerked the trigger again and a slug smashed into the youth's shoulder, splintering the bone and spinning him around in a blur of pain. Joe pitched forward

A Slug Hits Little Joe's Shoulder

on his knees, blood streaming down his shirt sleeve.

"I'm not here to play patty-cake!" hissed Apache Jack.

"What *are* ya here to play, ya lily-livered milksop?" exclaimed Hoss as he and Ben spun their heads around and stared down the rifle barrels held by the two grinning Indians, who were quietly padding toward them on horseback.

"Maybe a little mumblety-peg!" crackled the outlaw, whipping his bowie knife from its sheath and

"I'm Not Here to Play Patty-Cake!"

slicing it through the air toward Little Joe. It sunk to its hilt in the soft ground, pinning Little Joe's bloody shirt sleeve with it.

"Hop Sing!" bellowed Ben. "Come out of the cabin and bandage Little Joe's shoulder! These yellow-bellied varmints won't shoot you. It's me they're after!"

Hop Sing appeared in the door-way, frying pan in hand. Beads of sweat covered his face. "Don't shoot!" he whimpered. "Hop Sing harmless!"

Pinned to the Ground

"You didn't tell me they had a Chinese cook!" snarled Apache Jack at Buffalo Face. "Now we'll have to string *him* up, too!"

Buffalo Face shrugged his shoulders.

"What do ya mean—*string up?*" asked Hoss, clenching and un-clenching his fists.

Apache Jack threw back his head and snickered. Then he dismounted, his Winchester still pointed at the Cartwrights. Yellow Wolf and Buffalo Face also slid off their horses.

"String 'Em Up!"

"See this rope?" he asked. "We've got three of 'em. That means Ben, you, and Hop Sing are gonna dangle from a branch over there, while we take potshots at you!"

"But why?" asked Ben. "And what about Little Joe?"

"I'm gonna have the pleasure of scalpin' him alive!" exclaimed the rustler. "We ain't got enough ropes, 'n' he's conveniently pinned to the ground, anyway!" He jabbed the muzzle of his Winchester into Ben's stomach. "I've been waitin' for this

"See This Rope?"

chance for a long time, old man—
ever since you had me run out of
town." *

The Bubble Gum Kid slowed his
broken-down horse to a walk as he
approached an ice-cold mountain
stream. "Guess we're both pretty
dry!" he muttered as the cow pony
plunged its loose lips into the water.
While the bronco lapped away, the
Kid knelt down several feet up-
stream and drank deeply. He was
about to wipe off his mouth on his

The Kid Pauses for a Drink

sleeve when the flat crack of a gun being fired rattled through the pine trees.

"That was no six-shooter!" he exclaimed, rising to his feet. "That was a Winchester—'n' the Cartwrights don't *have* any Winchesters!" He automatically drummed his fingers on the Colt .45 dangling at his side. "Come on, old timer!" he shouted at the bewildered horse. "We've got work to do!"

Leaping awkwardly into the saddle, the Kid spun his mount about

"Come on, Old Timer!"

as a second shot echoed through the trees. "Git a goin'!" he urged, kicking his spurs into his horse's flanks and almost falling off in the process.

Approaching the outskirts of the Cartwright property, the Kid dismounted, hitched the horse to a rotted stump, then slid his Colt out of its holster and cocked it with a metallic click. Confusing sounds drifted to his ears, including what seemed to be the tortured moaning of an animal. He crept forward, careful not to step on dry twigs.

The Kid Creeps Forward

What he saw, when he parted the last screen of bushes, drained the blood from his face.

Hoss, Ben, and Hop Sing were straddling three horses—backward. Their hands were lashed behind them, and loose nooses were stretched from their necks to an overhead branch, where hard-breathing Yellow Wolf was busy fastening each rope with a half hitch. Little Joe lay spread-eagled in the dust, an oozing wound in one shoulder, a bowie knife pinning

The Cartwrights Are in Trouble

his shirt to the ground.

"Pa!"

Apache Jack wheeled in his tracks and fired blindly at him. The Kid didn't feel a white-hot bullet rip his left cheek, for the sudden roar of his own gun blotted out all reactions. The bullet that blasted from his peacemaker glanced off the case-hardened receiver of his foe's rifle, dashing it to the ground. Apache Jack grabbed for it, a curse forming on his chapped lips, and the Kid squeezed the trigger again,

The Kid's Gun Roars

this time shattering his enemy's clutching hand with a spinning slug.

The wild-eyed horses holding Hoss, Ben, and Hop Sing, terrified by the unexpected gunplay, surged forward, snapping the ropes tight around the three necks. Whipping a half-turn to the right, the Bubble Gum Kid severed the taut ropes with three lightning shots, and the would-be victims toppled heavily to the ground. "It sure pays to practice!" exclaimed the Kid.

The Horses Bolt in Fright

While Apache Jack scrambled toward the rear of the cabin, Buffalo Face squinted down his rifle sight at the Kid's tousled head. "Ha!" he grunted, squeezing the trigger. The gun failed to fire.

"Only got one shot left!" mumbled the Bubble Gum Kid, quickly plunking his remaining bullet into the renegade's fat stomach. "Now, it seems like there was another varmint perched in that tree!" he added, rapidly snapping open his gun's cylinder and cramming fresh

The Kid Reloads

bullets into its empty chambers. He stalked forward into the corral, squinting into the sun-dappled foliage, his gun ready to bark. Yellow Wolf had disappeared, however, his dim-witted mind unable to understand what was going on.

"Pa," said the Kid, pulling his knife from its sheath and carefully slicing through the noose around Ben's neck. Then, stretching to one side, he cut the ropes choking Hoss and Hop Sing.

"You 'n' I have a score to settle,

Ben Is Freed

junior," rasped Apache Jack's hoarse voice from the shadows behind the cabin. "You forget that I can shoot equally well with either hand!"

"Save your breath, you tinhorn bandit," said the Kid. "I'm gonna slam so many holes through you they'll be able to use you as a fishnet!" He sidled swiftly to the edge of the cabin. "Ready?"

"I'm ready," replied Apache Jack.

"We Have a Score to Settle!"

"Well, I'll Be!"

Chapter 9

SHOWDOWN

Breathing heavily as he flattened himself against the side of the cabin, the Bubble Gum Kid became aware for the first time of the searing pain in his left cheek. "Well, I'll be," he muttered softly, running his fingertips across the skin. They were covered with blood.

Crouching in the shadows on the

far side of the cabin, Apache Jack licked his lips with his tongue and quietly hefted his revolver in the hand that wasn't shattered.

"I thought you were hot coffee with a pistol!" taunted the Kid, bending over and stealthily creeping forward. "How come all ya did was peel some skin off my cheek?"

"You caught me off guard!" hissed Apache Jack's hoarse voice. "I *never* miss with a six-shooter or a knife! You'll be a stiff within five minutes, Kid!"

Taunting Each Other

Thirty feet away, Ben Cartwright stirred uneasily in the dust, then rubbed his raw throat with his thumb. He rolled over and stared at Hoss, whose eyes were slowly opening. "What happened, Hoss?" he mumbled.

"Looks like the Bubble Gum Kid showed up just in time," replied his enormous son, sitting up and shaking his head.

A rapid volley of shots shook shingles from the shack's roof. "You shoot like a little old woman,"

"What Happened, Hoss?"

they heard the Kid say in a strained voice. "Only *one* of those hit me!"

"They're shootin' it out on the other side of the cabin!" exclaimed Ben. "That's *my* job!"

"Relax, Pa," said Hoss in a troubled voice, a deep frown creasing his forehead. "They took yer gun away. Besides, if any hombre can take care of that greasy outcast, it's the Bubble Gum Kid!"

As if in answer to his praise, the Kid staggered backward into the glaring sunlight, then collapsed.

The Kid Staggers Backward

Apache Jack stepped gingerly from behind the edge of the cabin and loomed over the prostrate figure. Casually raising his revolver, he pointed it at the Kid's face. "I've got two shots left in this here round. One's for you, 'n' the other's for Hoss. I'll polish off Ben 'n' that cook with my bowie knife!"

Little Joe moaned softly.

"Ya almost spoiled all my fun," continued the renegade. "I've been plannin' these fireworks since I broke out of jail!"

Apache Jack Takes Aim

Suddenly sweeping one leg sideways like an alligator's tail, the Bubble Gum Kid knocked Apache Jack head over heels.

"Look at that!" exclaimed Hoss.

Now it was the Kid who towered over his crumpled-up opponent. "On yer feet!" he commanded. "I just wanted to get ya out here in the sunshine where I can see ya!"

"Don't kill him!" pleaded Ben. "Ya'll get more reward money— and be more of a hero—if ya haul him into town alive!"

A Surprising Development

"I stomp my own snakes," replied the Kid in a flat voice.

"But I don't have my gun!" sniveled Apache Jack.

"I'll take care of that little detail," answered the Kid, nuzzling the fallen revolver toward the outlaw's hand with the toe of one boot.

Apache Jack rose unsteadily to his feet, his revolver hand hanging straight down at his side. "You've got the drop on me," he protested.

"I'll take care of that little detail, too! Put yer gun in yer holster!"

The Kid Gives Jack a Break

Having no choice since the muzzle of the Kid's gun was burrowing into his ribs, Apache Jack slid his Colt into its leather pocket.

"You've got two shots left," observed the Bubble Gum Kid, "so I'll match ya, even stephen!" Snapping open the cylinder of the secondhand gun Little Joe had given him, he emptied it of all but two shells. "Now we're gonna have the kind of showdown they feature in Wild West Shows back East!"

Hoss and Ben rose to their feet,

"I'll Match Ya, Even Stephen!"

neither of them speaking. Hop Sing opened his eyes, saw that there was going to be more shooting, and hastily snapped them together again.

"Stay right where ya are!" the Kid warned. "Now I'm gonna drop my gun into my holster!"

The two men instinctively crouched down and began circling one another, each waiting for the other to make the first move. Heavy silence hung over the corral, broken only by the scraping sound of their boots shuffling through the dust.

Apache Jack Circles The Kid

Apache Jack backed up to the watering trough to get added support, his good hand trembling over the butt of his revolver. His cheek twitched as he calculated the lightning second when he would snap the gun from its pocket in a blurring motion and puncture the Kid's lungs.

The Kid, meanwhile, had stopped circling and now crouched completely motionless.

"*Now!*" thought Apache Jack to himself, his hand streaking toward

Ready to Draw

the notched gun at his side.

Four shots shattered the air simultaneously, followed by a resounding splash. Hoss and Ben sprang forward to tackle Apache Jack if he were still on his feet. He wasn't. The outlaw lay half-submerged in the water.

"Didn't even get his gun out of his holster!" exclaimed Hoss.

"Shot his own foot while trying to!" added Ben, hauling the drenched, semi-conscious outcast out of the trough.

Half-Submerged

The Kid thoughtfully tapped the muzzle of his gun against his chin. "I didn't kill him, Pa. I just winged him in both shoulders!"

Hoss and Ben dragged Apache Jack over to the buckboard and heaved him up on the back as though he were a sack of flour.

Ben turned to the shaggy-haired stripling. "Here, Kid, take this bum into town and collect your reward!"

"We'll follow you in the wagon, with Little Joe," added Hoss. "We've gotta get him to a doc."

'I Just Winged Him."

The Bubble Gum Kid swung up into the buckboard's seat, then stared down at the two Cartwrights. "I've been thinkin', Pa. Maybe I *will* hang around and chop wood for you. Mexico's a long way off!"

"Especially when you're ridin' a moose!" Hoss said with a grin.

Ben and the Kid exchanged a long, meaningful glance. "You're okay, Kid," Ben said finally. "And I've always wanted another son."

"Maybe I Will Hang Around!"

Other **BIG LITTLE BOOKS** Available

THE MAN FROM U.N.C.L.E.—The Calcutta Affair

DICK TRACY—Encounters Facey

BONANZA—The Bubble Gum Kid

FLIPPER—Killer Whale Trouble

LASSIE—Adventure in Alaska

TARZAN—The Mark of The Red Hyena

TOM and JERRY—Meet Mr. Fingers

BUGS BUNNY—Double Trouble on Diamond Island

POPEYE—Ghost Ship to Treasure Island

DONALD DUCK—The Fabulous Diamond Fountain

WOODY WOODPECKER—The Meteor Menace

THE INVADERS—Alien Missile Threat

WHITMAN *Tween-Age Books*

Easy to Read . . . Full of Fun and Adventure

Books About Animals

GOLDEN PRIZE—Stories About Horses

HERE, BOY!—Stories About Dogs

THAT'S OUR CLEO!—Stories About Cats

Old Favorites

TALES FROM THE ARABIAN NIGHTS

TALES FROM HANS CHRISTIAN ANDERSEN

Adventure

ADVENTURES WITH HAL

DONALD DUCK AND THE LOST MESA RANCH

DORY BOY

IT'S A MYSTERY!

MYSTERY AT REDTOP HILL

WHITMAN *Big Book Adventures*

Based on famous TV shows

I SPY

THE GREEN HORNET

THE MAN FROM U.N.C.L.E.

BONANZA

LASSIE

FLIPPER

THE BIG VALLEY

PATTY DUKE

GILLIGAN'S ISLAND

VOYAGE TO THE BOTTOM OF THE SEA